FISH FRY
TONIGHT

FISH FRY
TONIGHT

by Jackie French Koller
illustrated by Catharine O'Neill

CROWN PUBLISHERS, INC.
New York

To Molly Kate
with love,
Aunt Jackie
—J. F. K.

To Baby Jarrah,
without whose help
this could have been
done much faster
—C. O'N.

Text copyright © 1992 by Jackie French Koller
Illustrations copyright © 1992 by Catharine O'Neill

Published by Crown Publishers, Inc., a Random House company, 225 Park Avenue South, New York, New York 10003

CROWN is a trademark of Crown Publishers, Inc.
Manufactured in the United States of America

Library of Congress Cataloging-in-Publication Data
Koller, Jackie French.
Fish fry tonight / story by Jackie French Koller; pictures by Catharine O'Neill.
p.   cm.
Summary: A cumulative tale in which a small mouse catches a fish and brings home a large group of friends to help her eat it.
[1. Mice—Fiction. 2. Animals—Fiction.] I. O'Neill, Catharine, ill. II. Title.
PZ7.K833Fi   1992
[E]—dc20   89-49369
ISBN 0-517-57814-X (trade)
0-517-57815-8 (lib. bdg.)
10 9 8 7 6 5 4 3 2 1   First Edition

One day, on a bright,
sunny morning in May,
Mouse left her washing,
and all of her dishes,
and, dreaming of fishes,
ran off to her favorite
spot by the brook.

There she lay lazing,
contentedly gazing,
at ripples and dapples
that giggled and babbled.
While dozily drowsing,
she dangled a hook.

In a flash
came a splash!
And a terrible tug!
A fish—what a whopper,
a jigger, a bopper!
The rod was bent double!
Mouse…was in *trouble*.
"Help!" she cried. "Help!
There's a whale on my line!"
But no one could hear.
No one was near.
Mouse had to fight all alone.

So she dug in her feet
and she pulled on the rod,
and she lugged and she tugged,
and she strained and she groaned,
and she huffed and she puffed,
till that fish had enough.
Then with one final yank
it lay still on the bank.

"I did it!" Mouse shouted.
"I did it! I *won!*
I didn't give up
and I caught him!
What fun!
The biggest fish I've ever seen,
the fattest, the fiercest,
the finest! Yippee!
What a delight!
FISH FRY TONIGHT!"

Then Mouse took her fish
and she headed for home.
She packed it in ice
and she got on the phone.
"Squirrel," she said,
"just wait till you see.
I caught a fish
as B–I–G as me!

"So bring a friend.
Bring two or three!
I'd love to have
the company.
We'll dine at eight,
so don't be late."

"Hooray!" shouted Squirrel.
"You've got a date!"

Squirrel scurried over
to Willowbrook Glen,
where Rabbit was cooking
outside of his den.
"Welcome," said Rabbit.
"I hope you can stay.
I'm feeling a little bit
lonely today."

"Cheer up, then," said Squirrel.
"My news will delight you.
 We're having a party
 and I've come to invite you.
 Mouse caught a fish
 as B–I–G as me!
 She said bring a friend,
 or two, or three.
 Dinner's at eight,
 so don't be late."

"Yahoo!" shouted Rabbit.
"We'll celebrate!"

Rabbit hopped over
to Bayberry Town,
where Badger was digging
a hole in the ground.
"New back door," Badger boasted.
"Thirsty work, hungry too.
Be dang near starved
before I'm through."

"Good," Rabbit told him.
"You timed it just right,
'cause Mouse wants us all
to come over tonight.
She's caught a fish
as B–I–G as me.
She said bring a friend,
or two, or three.
We're dining at eight,
so don't be late."

"Well, swell!" shouted Badger.
"I can hardly wait."

On his way to the brook
to wash up after work,
Badger heard mumbling.
"Same thing," Deer was grumbling,
"day in and day out.
Stripping bark is so boring
I'm practically snoring."

"Humph," Badger snorted.
"*I* should have it so good,
but if you're that tired
of chewing on wood,
Mouse caught a fish
as B–I–G as me.
She said bring a friend,
or two, or three.
Chow's on at eight,
so *don't* be late."

"Splendid!" said Deer.
"That'll be first-rate!"

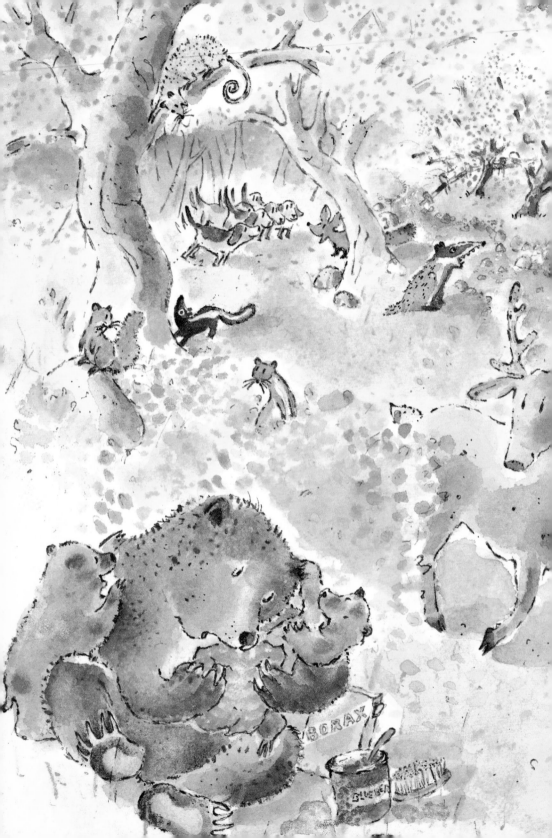

On her way through the forest
Deer came across Bear,
who was scrubbing her cubs
just outside of her lair.
"Berries," Bear muttered,
"on noses and paws.
Berries on cheeks,
on chins, and on claws…
Just once I wish
we could dine on a dish
that wouldn't turn cubs
into berry-stained grubs!"

"Pardon," said Deer,
"but Mouse has some fare
that she's willing to share.
She's caught a fish
as B–I–G as me.
She said bring a friend,
or two, or three.
I'm sure she won't mind
your whole family.
Come at eight,
and don't be late."

"Thanks!" shouted Bear.
"That sounds just great!"

At home Mouse was merrily,
busily bustling,
cleaning and cooking
and happily humming,
"Fish fry tonight!
My friends will be coming
precisely at eight.
Yippee, I can't wait!"

The table was set
with four extra places,
one was for Squirrel
and three "just-in-cases."
The candles were lit
as the clock started chiming,
"Bong, bong, bong, bong,
bong, bong, bong, bong."
DING-DONG! What timing!

Mouse yanked off her apron
and threw it aside,
then ran to the door
and opened it wide.

But then what she saw
nearly caused her to swoon,
for outside her door
in the light of the moon
stood not one or two friends,
not just a few friends…

but friends by the dozen!
Friends by the scad!
More friends than Mouse
ever knew that she had.

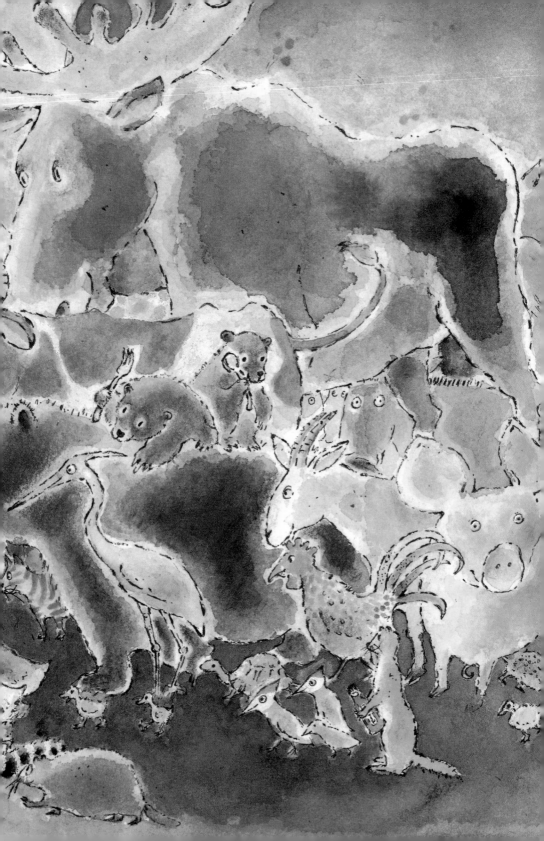

"Excuse me," she gasped,
"I'll just be a minute."
Then she closed the door
and leaned against it.
"No need to panic,"
she told herself.
"So things got a little
out of hand.
True friends will surely understand."

She ran to the phone
and ordered out,
"One hundred pizzas,
double cheese,
with *lots* of anchovies,
if you please."

Then taking a breath
to calm her nerves,
Mouse picked up a dish
heaped high with fish,
and went out to offer
her guests…

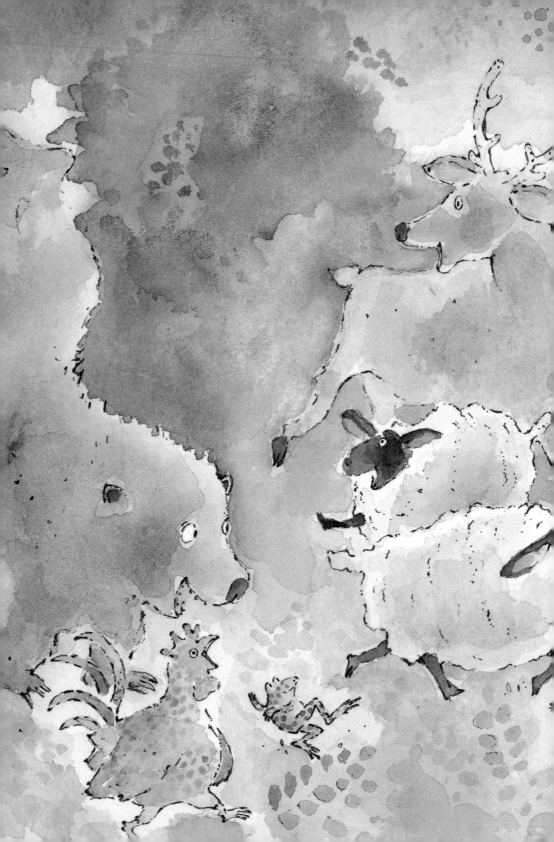

…hors d'oeuvres!
"Hooray!" they all yelled
when she came into sight.
"WHAT A DELIGHT!
FISH FRY TONIGHT!"

Mouse smiled.
"Well…," she said. "Yes…
more or less…"